Nell the Naughty Kitten

Tom bounded down the stairs, expecting the worst. And he was right. Nell was on the kitchen table. On the kitchen floor were one upturned tray and a couple of dozen smashed eggs.

"Oh, Nell, look what you've done!" gasped Tom, staring in horror at the oozing, slimy mess.

Titles in Jenny Dale's KITTEN TALES™ series

Titles in Jenny Dale's PUPPY TALES™ series

All of Jenny Dale's KITTEN TALES books can
be ordered at your local bookshop or are
available by post from Book Service by Post
(tel: 01624 675137)

Nell the Naughty Kitten

by Jenny Dale

Illustrated by Susan Hellard

A Working Partners Book

MACMILLAN CHILDREN'S BOOKS

Special thanks to Angie Sage

First published 1999 by Macmillan Children's Books
a division of Macmillan Publishers Limited
25 Eccleston Place, London SW1W 9NF
Basingstoke and Oxford
www.macmillan.com

Associated companies throughout the world

Created by Working Partners Ltd, London W6 0QT

ISBN 0 330 37454 0

7 9 8

A CIP catalogue record for this book is available from
the British Library.

Typeset by SX Composing DTP, Rayleigh, Essex
Printed and bound in Great Britain by Mackays of Chatham plc, Kent

Chapter One

"Tom quick, look! Nell's doing it again!" yelled Tom Morgan's twin sisters, Jo and Hattie.

Tom ran to the door and stared across the farmyard to the pigpen. A fat, squealing pig was tearing round the pen in a panic. Sitting calmly on the fence was a little stripy ball of fluff.

The ball of fluff was Nell, the new kitten on the farm.

"Oh no!" Tom pulled on his wellingtons and rushed out into the farmyard. Hattie and Jo ran after him.

Nell's favourite game was playing with the short, curly tail of Poppy, their heavily pregnant pig. But Poppy didn't seem to like this game very much.

Tom ran up to the pigpen just as Poppy skidded to a halt and stamped her trotters crossly. Nell jumped neatly down from the fence and landed at Tom's feet.

The kitten looked up at Tom and began to purr. He was her favourite person on the farm.

Tom picked Nell up, trying not
to smile. "You're a naughty girl!"
he said. "Poppy could have
squashed you!"

"It's not funny," said Hattie.

"No, it's not," agreed Jo. "You
know Poppy's expecting piglets
and she mustn't get upset. This is
the third time this week that
Nell's been inside her pen. Mum

will be really cross when she finds out."

Tom sighed. He knew Jo was right, but he found it hard to be angry with Nell. She was such *fun*! Much more interesting than his goldfish, Eric. Tom knew that Hattie and Jo loved Nell too, but not as much as he did.

"Well, we don't have to *tell* Mum," said Tom as he walked back to the house holding Nell tightly, just in case she decided to do something else naughty.

"I bet she'll know anyway," said Hattie. "Poppy won't stop squealing."

"Mum always knows if Poppy is upset," said Jo. "And she'll guess it was Nell again."

"But promise you won't tell her," shouted Tom over the noise of his mother's tractor coming into the farmyard.

"We won't," said Hattie and Jo.

Tom took Nell into the kitchen and put her into her basket. "Now you stay there," he said, trying to be stern. "Don't muck around any more today!"

Nell didn't like it when Tom was cross. "Can't we play with my toy mouse?" she miaowed.

But Tom still looked serious.

Nell sat back in her basket and yawned. She decided to give herself a bit of a wash. But before long, she fell asleep.

Tom got up and looked out of the window. He watched his

mum get down from the tractor and look into the pigpen. Hattie and Jo were shaking their heads solemnly.

"I hope Poppy's all right," Tom muttered to himself as his mum marched across the farmyard towards the kitchen.

The kitchen door opened and Mrs Morgan stomped into the house.

"Hi Mum," said Tom warily.

"Where's that cat?" replied Mrs Morgan.

"She's not a cat, Mum, she's only a kitten," said Tom. He went over to the cat basket where Nell was fast asleep.

"And she's too young to understand about pigs," said

Hattie, coming into the kitchen.

"And she's usually really good, isn't she, Tom?" added Jo.

"Yes, she is," said Tom. "She's just not used to being on a farm yet, that's all, Mum."

Mrs Morgan pulled off her boots and flopped down at the kitchen table. She looked tired. "Put the kettle on, Tom love," she said.

Tom filled the kettle with water and plugged it in.

Mrs Morgan wriggled her toes and put her feet up on a chair. "Well," she said, "I know Nell is only a kitten but she's come here to be a farm cat."

"I know, Mum," said Tom.

His mum carried on, "That means not jumping in the animal

feed. And not pulling straw out
of the bales. And not chasing
the ducks and pouncing on the
animals. Especially the pigs. And
especially Poppy."

"I know, Mum," Tom said again.
"Nell *will* learn to be a good farm
cat. I'm *sure* she will," he added,
crossing his fingers for luck.

The kettle boiled and Mrs

Morgan got up to make herself a cup of tea. She poured out some orange juice for Tom, Hattie and Jo and then sat down again, looking worried. "The thing is, I don't want Nell to upset Poppy again," she said. "Poppy is due to have her piglets next week, and if she's upset, she may not look after them properly."

Tom's heart thumped hard. Was his mum hinting that Nell might have to leave the farm? He had to think fast. "We could keep her inside until Poppy has had her piglets," he suggested. "She could stay in my bedroom. I'd make sure she stayed in – honestly Mum! And I'd feed her and empty her litter tray and look after her and—"

"All right," laughed Mrs Morgan. "You can keep Nell in your room until Poppy has had her piglets, OK?"

"Thanks, Mum!" Tom grinned. It would be great to have Nell sleep in his room. He often crept down to the kitchen at night to see if she was all right.

Tom picked up the cat basket and carefully carried it upstairs.

Nell stirred and gave a little miaow. In her dreams she was flying through the air.

Tom had just reached his bedroom door when Hattie bounded up behind him.

"It's not fair you having Nell," Hattie said, grabbing the basket.

"We want to have her too," said Jo, coming up behind Hattie.

"Well, Mum said she could go in *my* room," said Tom, trying to grab the basket back.

"No, in ours," his sisters hissed.

"Mine!"

"*Ours!*" Hattie tugged the basket and Nell tumbled onto the floor. She woke up with a start and shot off into Tom's room and hid under his bed.

"See. She likes my room the best anyway," said Tom.

"No she doesn't!" said Hattie crossly, still holding the basket.

"You just scared her, that's all," said Jo.

"Didn't."

"Did."

"*Stop it*, you three!" Mrs Morgan yelled up the stairs. "Tom, are you looking after that kitten?"

"Yes, Mum!" yelled Tom.

"Good!" shouted Mrs Morgan.

Hattie pushed the basket back at Tom and stuck her tongue out.

Tom crossed his eyes and if he

hadn't been holding the basket he would have stuck his fingers up his nose too. He waited until Hattie and Jo had clumped off downstairs and then he went into his room and closed the door.

He scooped Nell out from under his bed, brushed some fluff off her nose and cuddled her tightly. "You've got to be good from now on, Nell," he said.

"Miaow," replied Nell.

"I mean it," said Tom, trying to be stern again but not doing very well.

Nell saw Tom was smiling and licked his hand. She liked being in Tom's room. She snuggled down and went back to sleep.

Chapter Two

When Tom woke up the next morning he found Nell curled up on the pillow beside him. Suddenly there was a hammering on the door and Hattie and Jo burst into the room.

Tom sat up with a start and Nell hid under the duvet.

"There are *ten* of them!" shouted Hattie, dancing round the room.

"And they're so sweet!" yelled Jo as she leapt onto Tom's bed.

And they're so loud! thought Nell. She poked her nose out from under the duvet and sniffed. There was a smell around Jo and Hattie that reminded her of something. It reminded her of . . . PIG. Nell sneezed.

"Phew," said Tom to Hattie and Jo, "You both smell of . . ."

"*Piglets*!" said Jo.

"Piglets?" asked Tom. 'You mean Poppy's had her . . ."

"Piglets!" Hattie and Jo squealed like a couple of big piglets themselves. They rushed out of the bedroom and slammed

the door behind them.

Tom sighed and snuggled back
down in bed. Sometimes his
sisters were so noisy he wished
he had earplugs, or a soundproof
bedroom, or even better, a sister-
proof bedroom.

When he was sure that Hattie
and Jo had gone away, Tom got
out of bed. He wanted to see if

the piglets were all right. He was a bit worried that the piglets had arrived so early and hoped that it wasn't Nell's fault.

Tom got dressed, gave Eric some fish food and left Nell fast asleep on his pillow. He was soon outside in the morning sunshine.

"Morning, Tom." Mrs Morgan popped her head up over the wall of the pigpen.

"Morning, Mum!" said Tom. "Is Poppy OK?" he asked anxiously. "I mean, the piglets . . . well, they were early and I wondered if it was because of Nell . . ."

Tom's mum opened the gate to the pigpen for Tom to come in and look. She was smiling broadly. "They're all just fine,

Tom. I don't think Nell did any harm. Poppy probably had them early because it is such a big litter. She's never had so many piglets before and she's looking after them very well. Isn't she clever?"

Mrs Morgan bent down and stroked Poppy's head. Poppy snuffled and snorted while she lay on the straw feeding a long line of tiny, wriggling, pink piglets.

"Wow!" said Tom. "I've never *seen* so many piglets!"

"I'm really pleased," said Mrs Morgan proudly. "And how is Nell? Was she good last night?"

"Really good," said Tom. "I think she's going to behave from now on," he added hopefully. He

looked at the wriggling piglets lying close to their mum. They reminded him of when he had first seen Nell with all her brothers and sisters. They'd been gathered round their mum, a big tabby cat that lived on another farm.

Tom decided he'd better get

back to his room to see if she was still behaving herself. "I'll go and give Nell some breakfast, Mum," he said.

"OK, Tom," Mrs Morgan said. "But I think we need to keep Nell indoors today, until Poppy has got used to her new litter. Nell can come back out tomorrow."

"Great," said Tom, smiling happily. All he had to do was make sure Nell stayed out of trouble from now on. Easy! Tom thought as he walked back to the kitchen to get Nell's breakfast.

Impossible! he thought a few minutes later, when he opened his bedroom door. There was Nell, perched on the edge of a shelf just above the fish tank, staring at Eric.

Oh, no! Tom realised he must have left the lid off Eric's tank again.

Inside the fish tank was one very scared goldfish.

Nell was just dipping a paw into the water when she glanced up and saw Tom. "Hello," she miaowed. "Just doing a spot of fishing!"

"Nell!" yelled Tom. As soon as he said it he knew he shouldn't have.

Suddenly Nell forgot where her front paws were and they slipped and slid – then fell – straight into the fish tank. The rest of Nell followed. *Splash*!

Chapter Three

"Youuwwll!" Nell cried. The wet stuff was *horrible*.

Inside his underwater castle, Eric the goldfish had decided to play dead. For a goldfish, Eric was quite bright.

Tom ran over to the tank and scooped Nell out. Holding the

dripping kitten under one arm, Tom used his other hand to touch Eric gently.

Eric flicked his tail and shot out from his castle.

Tom breathed a sigh of relief, but was cross with himself. His mum was always telling him not to leave the lid off Eric's tank. He put the lid back on firmly, then went to the airing cupboard for an old towel to rub Nell dry.

"Thanks for rescuing me, Tom," Nell mewed weakly. She looked up at him, but Tom didn't smile. Nell felt miserable.

Tom wrapped Nell in a rather rough, threadbare towel then carried her down to the kitchen where it was warmer. "Cats are meant to be afraid of water, not jump into it!" he said sternly as he rubbed her dry. Nell looked very small and skinny with her wet fur.

Tom did smile then. "You look like a little rat," he said, "except I've never seen a tabby rat before."

Nell began to feel better. Her fur

felt warmer and less heavy. She yawned. All the excitement had made her tired, so she curled up in her towel and went to sleep.

Tom put Nell down by the radiator and was about to go and top up Eric's tank with water when Hattie and Jo came in, carrying two almost full trays of eggs from the hens.

"Look at all the eggs we got this morning. Forty-four!" said Hattie.

"Mum was really happy," said Jo.

They stacked them carefully on the table. "We're going out to see Poppy and her piglets now," they told Tom.

"OK," said Tom. He left Nell fast asleep by the radiator and shot off upstairs to sort out Eric.

Eric was fine. He was happily swimming around in about 10 centimetres of water, wondering what had happened to the rest of it. Eric had already forgotten about Nell falling in. Although Eric had a good memory for a goldfish, he still forgot *everything* after about five minutes.

Tom filled up the fish tank, gave Eric some more fish food and made sure he put the lid on. Then he heard the crash.

Tom bounded down the stairs, expecting the worst. And he was right. Nell was on the kitchen table. On the kitchen floor were one upturned tray and a couple of dozen smashed eggs.

"Oh, Nell, look what you've

done!" gasped Tom, staring in horror at the oozing, slimy mess.

Nell looked at Tom's face and thought she'd better get off the table. As she sprang down, Hattie burst into the kitchen.

"Mum wants her coat— aagh!" Hattie skidded on the eggs and banged right into the draining board. A glass and two cereal bowls toppled to the floor with a clatter as Hattie came to a halt.

"Oh no," groaned Tom.

"What a mess!" shouted Mrs Morgan when she ran in to see what was happening. "What has been going on?"

"Wow!" breathed Jo as she rushed in too, not wanting to be left out.

Nell sat crouched in the corner on her threadbare towel and looked at Tom's mum.

Tom's mum looked at Nell. "Did Nell do this?" she demanded.

"Not all of it," miaowed Nell, beginning to lick her paws, which were sticky with egg. All this noise and fuss – she wished more than anything that she was still safely asleep in her basket up in Tom's room.

"Well, Tom? Did she?" asked Mrs Morgan sternly.

"Sort of . . . I suppose . . ." Tom said reluctantly.

"I thought so," said his mum. "That kitten is nothing but trouble! I don't think she'll ever make a good farm cat. We won't have a farm left if she carries on like this!" Mrs Morgan sighed. "I really think Nell may have to go and live somewhere else," she said quietly.

"No, Mum!" cried Tom.

Nell looked down at her eggy paws, feeling very miserable.

"But Mum, Nell didn't break the crockery," said Hattie. "I knocked it all on the floor when I slipped on the eggs."

"And I'm sure Nell didn't *mean* to break the eggs, Mum," said Tom. "Please give her another chance. *Please*!"

"Please!" said Hattie and Jo.

Mrs Morgan looked at the three pleading faces. "All right," she said, sighing again. "One more chance. Just one! But that's it, OK?"

"OK, Mum," said Tom, smiling in relief.

While Hattie and Jo helped Tom clear up the broken eggs and smashed crockery, Mrs Morgan went out to feed the pigs.

Nell sat quietly under the radiator and carried on cleaning her paws.

The kitchen was soon clean and tidy again. Hattie and Jo ran off outside to play.

Tom decided he ought to try and get back in his mum's good books. He'd go and help her with the pigs. "Back soon, Nell," he said. "Be good."

Nell stopped licking her paws and watched the door close behind Tom. Then she watched it swing open again as it came off the latch.

Nell sat and looked at the slight opening in the kitchen door. Her nose twitched. It was such a lovely warm day and the farmyard sent such interesting smells wafting her way.

She sat there a bit longer. Then she decided. She could be just as good sitting by the open door, couldn't she? She crept over to the doorway and poked her little pink nose out into the sunshine . . .

Chapter Four

Over in Poppy's pen, Tom and his mum were giving Poppy and her piglets some clean straw to lie on. Suddenly a burst of squawking came from the duck pond.

Tom's heart thumped quickly. Nell! He rushed out just in time to see Nell scooting round the pond, chasing all the ducks into the water. He caught the naughty kitten almost at once, but by then Tom's mum had seen what had happened.

"I'll take Nell inside and shut her in my room," said Tom quickly.

Mrs Morgan nodded crossly. "And make sure she stays there this time," she snapped. "I've had

quite enough of that kitten today."

Nell could tell that she was in trouble again. Tom took her up to his room and played with her for a while, but Nell could see that he was thinking about something else. After a while, she went over to snooze in the warm sunshine by the window.

Nell was right, Tom *was* thinking about something. He was thinking about Nell's last chance and hoping that his mum did not mean what she had said.

But that evening, when Tom was on his way to clean his teeth, he heard his mum and dad talking in the kitchen.

"Tom will be very upset," Tom's

dad was saying. "He's become especially fond of Nell."

"I know," sighed Tom's mum, "but that kitten is never going to settle down here. It would be kinder to let Julie take Nell now so that she can get used to a new home while she's still young."

"Maybe . . ." said Mr Morgan. "But let's give it just a little bit longer, just for Tom."

"You're a big softie," Tom heard his mum say. "OK, one last chance, then."

Tom rushed back to Nell. He picked her up and hugged her tightly. "From now on you really, *really* have to stop being so naughty, Nell," he told her. "Otherwise you have to go and live with Auntie Julie."

Nell was having a strange dream about being hugged by a talking pig. She gave a muffled miaow.

Tom smiled. He loved Auntie Julie, but there was no way she was going to have Nell . . .

The next day was hot and sunny. Tom's mum and dad were busy up in the fields turning the hay so that it dried in the sunshine.

Nell was sitting quietly on Tom's windowsill, gazing out at the sunny farmyard. She stuck her pink nose right up against the window and wished she was outside too, having fun.

Her eyes followed Tom as he

walked up to the field where Mr
and Mrs Morgan were working.
Nell could see Hattie and Jo in
the far corner of the field, where
they were allowed to play with
the hay. They had built a big pile
and were jumping into it. It
looked like fun!

And now Tom was joining in. Nell yawned and stretched. She wanted some fun too!

She jumped down from the windowsill and went downstairs to explore. But the kitchen door was firmly shut. And so was the door to the sitting-room.

Nell scampered back upstairs. She looked in the bathroom. Nothing much to play with in there. The next room she came to looked far more interesting . . .

When lunchtime arrived, Mrs Morgan called Tom, Hattie and Jo over. "Hay monsters!" she laughed, as they arrived, picking bits of hay out of their hair and clothes.

"Can I let Nell out for a while, Mum?" Tom asked, as they all walked back to the house together. "I'll stand and watch her, to make sure she doesn't get into any trouble."

Mrs Morgan nodded. "As long as you *do* watch her," she said.

Tom smiled back then glanced up at his bedroom window to see if Nell was still looking out. There was no sign of her. Then something caught his eye in the next window along, his mum and dad's bedroom. Tom couldn't quite believe what he saw. Outside it was beautiful sunshine, but inside his mum and dad's room it was snowing.

Chapter Five

"What on earth . . . ?" gasped Mrs Morgan. She had seen it too and began to rush towards the house.

Tom hurried behind her with his dad and sisters. He had an awful feeling that this was something to do with Nell . . .

Mrs Morgan marched through

the kitchen and up the stairs with Tom hot on her heels. She threw open the bedroom door.

Tom squeezed past her into the room. He was right. There in the middle of the big bed, surrounded by a cloud of white feathers, was Nell. She was busily shaking a pillow as though it was a huge white mouse. The other pillow looked crumpled and empty – its feathers already floating around the room.

Nell looked up, saw Tom and was about to purr – but sneezed instead. Then she saw Tom's mum. Mrs Morgan's face was very red and fierce-looking. Nell knew that she was in big trouble. She jumped off the bed, shot out

of the room and hid in her basket in Tom's bedroom.

"They're my best pillows. I don't believe it. I just don't!" shouted Mrs Morgan.

"Mum, please, she was bored," Tom pleaded. "I should have left her a toy to play with."

"No, Tom," Mrs Morgan replied. "She's just too naughty and this is the last straw!"

Nell sat in her basket and listened miserably to the fuss going on next door. Soon she heard the sound of Mrs Morgan's footsteps going downstairs. Then Tom came in and picked her up.

"Oh, Nell!" he said sadly. "You've really done it this time.

Mum's on the phone to Auntie Julie."

Mrs Morgan's voice came floating up the stairs. "I'm so cross! I'm going to have to buy new pillows, Julie . . ." she was saying. "Yes, terrible . . . Tomorrow morning will be fine . . . Thanks, Julie . . . Bye . . . Bye . . ."

Tom sighed and Nell noticed his eyes looked all wet.

Tom didn't want to talk to Auntie Julie when she arrived the next morning.

"Hello, Tom," she said. "I'm really sorry about Nell. You know that you can come and see her any time, don't you? Any time at all."

Tom stared at his feet. It wasn't that he didn't like Auntie Julie. The trouble was that he liked her very much and if she was any nicer to him he had an awful feeling that he might cry. So he kept staring at his feet and said nothing.

"Hattie, Jo," said Mrs Morgan,

"why don't you show Auntie Julie the new piglets while Tom says goodbye to Nell?"

"What a good idea," said Auntie Julie, sounding pleased to get out of the kitchen. She ushered Hattie and Jo out of the door.

"Right," said Tom's mum when they had gone. "Let's find Nell and you can say goodbye to her properly."

Tom didn't say anything.

"Come on, love," said Mrs Morgan. "Surely you can see that Nell can't stay? And she's only going down the road. You can see her every day at Auntie Julie's if you want to."

"But it won't be the same," Tom mumbled at his shoes.

Mrs Morgan sighed, but she wasn't going to change her mind this time. "Now, where is she?" she asked.

With a heavy heart, Tom went up to his room to fetch Nell. He had left her asleep on his bed when he came downstairs that morning.

But Nell wasn't there. She had gone.

Ten minutes later they still hadn't found Nell.

Tom's mum was getting annoyed. "Are you hiding that kitten somewhere?" she asked Tom.

"No," Tom replied truthfully. It was a good idea and he wished he'd thought of it, but he had no idea where Nell was either.

Crossly, Mrs Morgan called Hattie and Jo in to help search for Nell. Soon they were turning the house upside down.

"She's been here," called out Hattie, "'cos my drawing paper's got footprints on it."

"And here," said Jo. "Look, she's eaten my chocolate."

"You ate that yourself, silly," said Hattie, scornfully.

Tom was beginning to wonder if Nell really had disappeared.

Chapter Six

Out by the pigpen, huddled inside an upturned tin bucket, Nell kept as quiet as a mouse. When Mrs Morgan had taken her basket out of Tom's room that morning, Nell had guessed that something not very nice was going to happen to her.

Nell had crept downstairs, and when Tom's Auntie Julie had arrived, she had scooted outside unnoticed. She watched and waited, listening unhappily to the sounds going on around her.

"We can't find her anywhere," sighed Hattie and Jo.

Tom watched Auntie Julie through the window as she fussed around the pigpen. He was beginning to hope that Nell would disappear long enough for Auntie Julie to give up waiting and go home. He threw himself down on the sofa and sighed.

A moment later Auntie Julie came back in. Mrs Morgan shook

her head to let her know that they hadn't found Nell.

Auntie Julie shrugged her shoulders, then sat down at the kitchen table.

"You can't hide Nell forever," Mrs Morgan told Tom crossly.

"I'm *not* hiding her!" Tom cried.

Out by the pigpen, Nell's nose twitched. Something was wrong. She peeped around the edge of the bucket and saw a little pink bottom with a curly tail rush by. It was one of the piglets. What was it doing out of the pigpen?

Nell crept out of the bucket to see more piglets running from the pen, while their mother snuffled about in the chicken feed. The

pigpen gate hadn't been closed
properly. As she watched, one of
the piglets squeezed under the
front gate and ran down the lane.

Nell was worried. She liked to
tease the other farm animals, but
she didn't want to see any of
them hurt. And that piglet was
going to get into big trouble,
running off like that!

Nell dashed over to the house – but the kitchen door was closed! She jumped onto the stone ledge under the kitchen window. Tom and his sisters, and his mum and Auntie Julie were all sitting round the table, talking.

"Tom! Tom – come out! Come and look!" Nell miaowed loudly, scratching on the windowpane as she called.

Everyone looked up.

"Catch her!" shouted Mrs Morgan, pushing her chair back and dashing outside, closely followed by Tom.

Then Mrs Morgan saw that the piglets were out of their pen. "Oh no!" she cried, forgetting about Nell. "Catch them!" she yelled.

Everyone began to run around the yard, herding the piglets safely back into the pen. But Nell ran over to the front gate, hoping Tom would follow her.

"Come here, Nell," Tom called, walking towards her.

But Nell ran under the gate and on down the lane.

"Nell! Come back!" Tom called. He quickly climbed over the gate and ran after her.

Just then, Nell spotted the runaway piglet snuffling about in a muddy ditch. She stood there, waiting for Tom to catch up.

At first, Tom couldn't believe his eyes. Nell wasn't being naughty at all. She'd run off to show him one of the farm animals was in trouble!

When Tom's mum spotted him walking back up the lane she called out to him, looking worried. "There's a piglet missing, Tom."

"No there isn't," Tom called back, smiling. He held the piglet up for his mum to see.

Nell walked beside Tom, feeling pleased. Perhaps she was a real farm cat now.

But Mrs Morgan didn't see it that way. She briskly picked Nell up and tucked her under her arm. "I might have known you'd be right in the middle of trouble," she said to Nell crossly.

"Mum . . ." protested Tom.

"Oh, that's not fair," Auntie Julie told her sister. "All this was my fault, not Nell's."

"Your fault?" asked Mrs Morgan, puzzled.

Auntie Julie went a little pink. "I must have left the pigpen gate open. Sorry."

"And Mum," said Tom, "if Nell hadn't come and scratched on the window at us, all the piglets might have got out on the road!"

"Oh don't, Tom," said Mrs Morgan, looking pale.

"So Nell wasn't being naughty at all this time," Jo said brightly.

Tom smiled at his sister. "That's right. Nell knew what was happening, Mum," he said. "She came and got us – and then she led me straight to the piglet that had run off down the lane!"

"Now Nell's a proper farm cat," said Harriet, happily.

"So I think we should keep her, Mum," Tom said quietly.

Harriet and Jo nodded hard.

Mrs Morgan looked at Auntie Julie to see what she thought.

"Tom's right," said Auntie Julie.

"I think Nell will be a good farm cat, after all."

"Yes, I will," miaowed Nell, wriggling in Mrs Morgan's arms. "Now can you stop squashing me, please?"

Mrs Morgan untucked the wriggling kitten from under her arm and gave her to Tom, smiling. "Then I suppose she can stay."

"*Really*?" asked Tom.

"Really," laughed Mrs Morgan.

Hattie and Jo cheered and Tom hugged Nell tight, a huge smile on his face.

As Nell purred happily in Tom's arms, two ducks waddled past. Nell's tail twitched. She was tempted, but she wasn't going to chase them. No – she was going to enjoy being a good farm cat – for today, at least . . .